A Sea of Stories

To Joke, the perfect partner
for an adventure – PD

STRIPES PUBLISHING LIMITED
An imprint of the Little Tiger Group
1 Coda Studios, 189 Munster Road, London SW6 6AW

First published in Great Britain in 2019

Text copyright © Sylvia Bishop, 2019
Illustrations © Paddy Donnelly, 2019

ISBN: 978-1-78895-081-7

Printed and bound in China.

STP/1800/0263/0419

2 4 6 8 10 9 7 5 3 1

A Sea of Stories

Sylvia Bishop

Illustrated by
Paddy Donnelly

STRIPES

Roo's grandpa lived in a cottage by the sea,
with his ancient cat, Bathsheba.
Outside, it was very beautiful.

Inside, it was a bit of a mess. Grandpa had a huge collection of Bits-and-Pieces, which he had been collecting since he was a small boy.

Roo's mum would smile, and say, "Grandpa, you are keeping the whole world in this cottage."

This summer, Roo was staying with Grandpa by herself.

"Have a lovely time," said Mum, giving her an enormous hug.

"Be good – ARGH! Oh dear. Sorry," said Dad, tripping over an old trunk. Roo's dad did not get on very well with Grandpa's Bits-and-Pieces.

"Goodbye, Roo," her parents said. "We'll see you in a few days!"

Roo felt a bit strange once her parents had gone, so she hugged Grandpa, then hurried upstairs to make her room feel like home. From the blue room, where she always stayed, she could see a silvery strip of sea.

The window was open, letting in the scents of the garden and the salty smell of the seaside.

Grandpa came up to Roo's room, and asked what he always asked:

"So what are we doing today, Roo?"

"Could we go to the cove?"

The cove was a little beach that hardly anybody knew about, hidden in the wriggle of a cliff.

Roo's mother had played there with Grandpa and Grandma when she was little, and Roo's parents would take her there whenever they visited Grandpa.

"I'm afraid we can't go to the cove, Roo," said Grandpa. "I'm not able to get down that rambly-scrambly path these days."

Roo tried not to look too disappointed. Grandpa had to walk very carefully, leaning on a stick, and she could see that it would be difficult for him.

"Sorry, Roo," said Grandpa. "How about some hide-and-seek in the garden instead? And later I can tell you a story or two about the cove that you won't believe!"

So all morning they played hide-and-seek.

The garden had been planted with beautiful flowers when Grandma was alive. Now that Grandpa was too old to look after it, it had grown tall and tangled and wild, with lots of places to hide.

Roo was wearing a raincoat. It had rained in the night and if you weren't careful, one of the wild and tangly plants might give you a shower.

Roo's hiding places
got better and better,
until she found such a
good one that Grandpa
couldn't find her at all.

"I give in!" he called.
"Where on *earth* are
you, Roo?"

When Grandpa was too tired for more
hide-and-seek, they went inside and he
settled into his favourite armchair.

"Now, Roo. Pick anything you like from
those shelves above the fireplace, and I'll
tell you the story behind it."

Nestled between a glove and a birdcage,
something golden winked at her.

"What's this one, Grandpa?" she asked, fetching it down. It was a small, heavy piece of gold, the size of Roo's palm.

"Aha! That is your Grandpa's own pirate treasure. I found that doubloon," said Grandpa, grinning, "in Sailor's Cave."

Roo stared at Grandpa. Sailor's Cave was in the cove, just past the rambly-scrambly path, but she had never been inside. It was said to be haunted by the ghosts of sailors drowned at sea, who had wide, staring eyes and seaweed for hair.

"What were you doing in the cave?" she said.

Grandpa smiled. "Good question…"

"It was the summer holidays, and I was not much older than you are now. Jim and I – you know my old friend Jim, who lives next door – we had a new game. We would both bury some treasure, then give each other directions to it in code. Whoever was the first to find their treasure won the game.

I had never lost. This was partly because your Grandpa is clever and noble and brave, but to be honest, it was also because Jim was not brilliant at hiding things.

But this particular day, I was struggling. I had been searching for hours.

The sun was starting to sink down below the sea when at last I cracked it:

Jim had hidden his treasure in Sailor's Cave.

You will remember, of course, that your Grandpa is clever and noble and brave – most *especially* brave. So, of course, I had to go in and find it, ghosts or no ghosts.

The evening light lay long and low on the beach, but in the cave, it was dark. The air inside was damp and chill, and the floor was slippery. With every step, my feet made a *shluck-shluck-shluck*ing sound.

I walked on. *Shluck-shluck-shluuuuck.*

Your Grandpa is *very* brave.

But then, a little way in, I slipped,
and sploshed into a pool full of wriggly
cold *something* that clung to my hair and
clothes and skin.

Your Grandpa is most *extraordinarily*
brave, but by now I was also wet and
slime-covered and ready to go home.

As I stumbled away, I nearly tripped over a box sitting on the ground. Jim's treasure!

I was about to pick it up when I heard them…

Through the darkness, footsteps were *shluck-shluck-shluck*ing towards me, closer and closer. The ghosts of sailors drowned at sea!

Suddenly there was a light, shining right into my face.

"Argh!" I yelled.

"Arrrrrgh! The ghost-of-a-sailor-drowned-at-sea!" yelled Someone Else.

Which seemed like an odd thing for the ghost-of-a-sailor-drowned-at-sea to say.

"Run!" said another voice.

As they ran, they dropped the torch. I shone it after them. Not ghosts at all. Ordinary men. Frightened away by a boy with seaweed in his hair and wild staring eyes.

When they were gone, I heaved Jim's treasure box up from the ground and hurried home. But when I opened it, it wasn't Jim's treasure at all. It was *real* treasure!

I showed my parents and they recognized it at once. They had heard about it on the news that morning! It had all been stolen from Hawberry Manor."

Roo knew Hawberry Manor. It was a very old house at the edge of Grandpa's town.

"So the men in the cave were the thieves?" said Roo.

"Yes! They had hidden their loot in the cave and were hoping to smuggle it away in the night."

"We took the box up to Lord and Lady Hawberry, who were so pleased that they gave me that doubloon to keep.

So that, Roo, is the story of your Grandpa's own pirate treasure. I never did find Jim's treasure – he had forgotten to hide it."

Bathsheba slunk on to Roo's lap and looked at the winking doubloon. She gave it a cautious lick …

wrinkled her nose …

and yawned,

showing her pink tongue.

Grandpa laughed. "It'll take more than pirate treasure to impress Bathsheba."

It was strange for Roo to think of Grandpa being her age, playing games with his friend Jim. She thought about it all through hide-and-seek the next day, as she listened to Grandpa's careful footsteps. It was hard to imagine him slipping and sliding around in Sailor's Cave.

When Grandpa grew tired, they went back inside.

"Can we have another story from when you were little?" Roo asked.

Grandpa nodded, scanning the Bits-and-Pieces.

"See the brass telescope, Roo? Fetch that down."

Roo did. It was heavy, and very beautiful. "Where did you get *this*, Grandpa?"

Grandpa smiled. "Good question," he said.

"My twelfth birthday was a magnificent birthday for two reasons. First, I had been given a telescope – but not the one you're holding now. Second, I was finally old enough to go out fishing at dawn, with my father and the other fishermen who crewed the *Pearl*.

I had been awake all night, imagining the
rocking of the boat and the sea spray and the hot
breakfast we would eat together as everybody else
woke up. Now it was finally time.

One of the *Pearl*'s crew, Bill Tubbs, was late.
Bill Tubbs, my father explained with a sigh,
was always late. While we waited, I played
with my new telescope.

There were
the other
boats out
at sea.

There were the
gulls overhead.

There was the grass on the clifftop.

That's when I saw the puppy.

At the very top of the cliff, the edge was lined
with thick bracken, and there was a puppy
that had got itself stuck. It was small, even
through my telescope, and I only spotted it
because it was wriggling so much. I wished
I could tell it to stop wriggling. One too-
wriggly wriggle could send it over the edge.

I told my father what I'd seen and asked if the crew could wait while I went to rescue it. But Bill had finally turned up, with ten different excuses and his jumper on back-to-front, and they had to get out to sea.

"You can go and rescue him, if you like," said my dad. "There'll be another boat tomorrow. It's up to you, boy."

The thought of the boat leaving without me made me miserable. But you will remember, Roo, that your Grandpa is clever and brave and noble – most *especially* noble – and I couldn't leave that puppy stranded.

So I set off.

At least I still had my telescope. Halfway up the cliff path, I paused to look at the fishing boats, and wonder which one was the *Pearl*.

It was a long way to the top and I was tired out by the time I reached the puppy. He was damp and frozen and hungry.

As I wrestled him free of the bracken, he wriggled and wriggled and wriggled, and I dropped my telescope … right over the cliff edge, with a clatter and a *smash*.

"You've caused me a lot of
trouble, dog," I said.

But he just shivered, and it is hard
to be angry with a shivering puppy.

I looked at him more closely. It was not any
of the dogs that I knew from the village.

"Well," I said. "We'd better find your home."

So I did. I went door to door, looking for his owner. And I found her! Anna Tippen nearly cried when she saw her runaway pup."

"Anna Tippen?" said Roo. "I know her! She runs the chip shop in Market Square!"

"Yes," said Grandpa. "In those days the shop was run by her parents. And when they heard how I'd broken my new telescope, they bought me that beautiful brass one to say thank you."

Bathsheba slunk on to Roo's lap, and looked at the telescope, head on one side. Roo held it up to the cat's eye…

Bathsheba was so surprised by what she saw, she tumbled off Roo's lap in a flurry of fur and paws!

Grandpa laughed. "I don't think cats like telescopes." He stood up. "All this talk is making me hungry. Let's get some chips!"

On Roo's last day at the cottage, the rain poured down and it was too wet to play hide-and-seek.

Instead, Roo played with the buttons from Grandma's old button box, arranging them into pictures and patterns. She hardly had any memories of Grandma, but she *did* remember them playing together with those buttons.

"Tell me about Grandma, Grandpa,"
Roo said, when it was time for a story.

Grandpa smiled, and considered his Bits-and-Pieces. Then he pointed to an old fishing net.

"My lucky net, Roo," he said.

Roo fetched the net.
It was vast and limp and smelly.

Bathsheba climbed on to Roo's lap
and sniffed it uncertainly.

"What's lucky about it?" Roo asked.

Grandpa smiled. "Good question," he said.

"When I was a young man, I went out fishing on the *Pearl* every morning. I complained about Bill Tubbs being late every morning and I ate my hot breakfast every morning as the town woke up. That day, Bill's daughter Laura was having *her* first outing on the boat.

It was a windy winter day and our boat was taking a beating, soaring up on the waves and crashing back down again.

As for poor Laura, her breath was as choppy as the sea and her face as pale as the winter sky. She was clutching a teddy bear that she had brought very tightly.

Then there was an extra-wild wave and we came down with such a *crash* that she dropped the bear overboard!

I leaned over the side to try and fish it out but it kept bobbing just out of reach. I was concentrating so hard on the bear that when we hit another wild wave, I was tipped right overboard!

Oh, that sea, Roo! It filled my eyes and ears and nose and mouth, and the cold cut right through me. The crew tried to help me, but the boat was being pulled away. I started to sink. Down…

down…

down…

And then suddenly, I sank *upwards*, which is not how sinking is supposed to work.

As I rose out of the water, I heard a voice saying, "Well, *that's* not a fish."

I had been caught in another boat's net!

The woman who untangled me from the net had eyes as wild as the sea. It was Alice. Your Grandma, Roo. She caught me in that very net you're holding now. And I can tell you, I didn't feel too brave or noble or clever – most *especially* not clever.

She laughed and laughed and laughed.

And she'd caught the teddy bear, too. So it really is a lucky net."

Roo held the mucky old net carefully.

"I always thought you and Grandma were in the same crew, Grandpa?"

Grandpa nodded. "We were," he said. "After your mother was born." He pointed to a big brass bell. "There's the bell from our boat: the *Mary Jane*."

"And you used to take Mum with you?"

Grandpa nodded again, and pointed to some wellies. "She wore those on her first trip."

"And did you go to our cove?"

"We went to the cove every evening," said Grandpa, "to watch the sun set."

But this time he didn't point at anything.

"Which of the Bits-and-Pieces is about the sunsets?"

"None of them, Roo. You can't keep a sunset indoors." Grandpa tapped his head. "But it's all in here."

Roo realized that her mum was wrong. Grandpa wasn't keeping the whole world in his cottage – not even close. He was cut off from the place he loved best.

She wished that she could find a way to bring the cove inside for him, with its sunrises and sunsets, and its cliffs and caves and sea.

That night, as she lay in bed, she didn't stop wishing.

The next morning, Roo
woke to find that her wish
had turned into a Plan.

For a minute she stayed
tucked up in her duvet
and wrote a list. Then she
packed up her things and
waited for her parents.

At last, the doorbell rang.

"Hello, Roo! Hello, Grandpa!" said her mum.

"Hello – arrrgh, oh, BOTHER," said her dad.

Her parents asked all the things that parents ask – about whether Roo had enjoyed herself and whether she had been good and whether she was sure she had remembered to pack everything.

Finally Roo hugged Grandpa goodbye.

"Mum," said Roo, as soon as they were in the car. "Dad. I've got an idea."

"Oh, yes?" said her parents cautiously.

"Could we clear up the rambly-scrambly path to the cove? So that Grandpa can go there again? I think he misses it a lot."

Her parents looked at each other.

"Well, it's a lovely idea, Roo," said her mum. "But we couldn't manage it by ourselves. It would take days of hard work."

"It wouldn't just be us," she said. "I'm sure these people will help us." And she read out her list:

Jim from next door
The Hawberrys
The Tippens from the chip shop
The Tubbs family
The crew of the MARY JANE

Her parents looked at each other again.

"*Please*," said Roo. "I want him to see the sunset there again."

"Oh," said Roo's mum, a far-off look on her face. "There's no better place for a sunset than that cove."

Roo's dad looked at Roo's mum and Roo, then rolled his eyes.

"Well, that's that then, isn't it?" he said, smiling.

They parked the car in the Market Square, and went to ask for help. Before long a great crew of people had assembled, carrying spades and buckets and wood and rope and tools of all sorts and sizes.

They cleared away bracken and brambles.

They shovelled away rocks and shingle.

Jim hung a rope handrail along the path.

Laura Tubbs put down wooden planks where it often got muddy and Anna Tippen put in crates for steps where you had to jump down between rocks.

The Hawberries brought a beautiful bench from their garden to put at the foot of the path.

"We thought there ought to be something in memory of your grandma," they said.

By the time they had finished, the sun was close to setting.

"Quick!" said Roo. "Let's fetch Grandpa!"

So Roo and her parents and Jim and the Hawberries and the Tippens and the Tubbses and all the crew of the *Mary Jane* went to knock on Grandpa's door.

"What's all this?" said Grandpa, blinking in surprise.

"One of Roo's ideas," explained Dad.

"Come and see, Grandpa!" said Roo, hopping impatiently from foot to foot.

Grandpa fetched his stick and followed them
to the top of the rambly-scrambly path.

When he saw what they had done, he was
speechless.

"*Meeeooow*," said a voice by his ankles – and
Bathsheba shot off down the path, purring.

Grandpa laughed. "You finally impressed
Bathsheba!" And he followed his
cat down to the cove.

Bathsheba curled up straight away on Grandma's bench.

Grandpa breathed very deeply – as if he was trying to fill himself right up to the brim with salty sea air.

"Thank you, Roo," he said at last. "It's *perfect*."

The light was long and low on the beach,
and it was quiet besides the *shhh-shhhhh* of the sea.
Together, they all watched the colours in the sky
over their cove, as the sun set below the waves.

ALICE GLENN

The End